MIRCEA VASILIU

MORTIMER,

THE FRIENDLY DRAGON

The **JOHN DAY** Company

New York

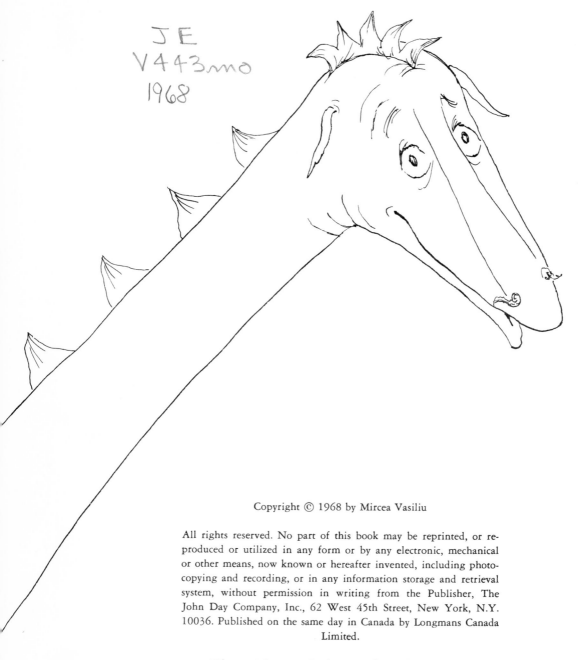

MORTIMER,
THE FRIENDLY DRAGON

One summer day a boy named Chris was walking through the park. He was looking for chipmunks, which he liked to watch, and also for birds and squirrels. Suddenly he stopped in his tracks. Right in front of him, sitting on a large rock next to a pond, was a dragon, and there was no one else around. Chris was petrified. But then the dragon

8

blinked a little and said in a soft voice, "Don't be petrified, because I am quite harmless."

"You mean you won't eat me up?" asked Chris.

"No, I am a vegetarian. I eat mostly grass, preferably when it is fresh, and also some fruit and vegetables, and I like people, but they don't usually like me," said the dragon.

"Maybe we could be friends," said Chris, who had one friend, Jonathan, and sometimes Peter, but not always.

"Nothing I would like better," said the dragon.

"My name is Christopher, but you can call me Chris," said Chris.

"My name is Mortimer, and people always call me Mortimer, but if you prefer, you can call me anything you like," said Mortimer.

"I will try, but if my tongue gets tired, I will call you Mort," said Chris.

"Would you care to take a walk?" asked Mortimer, and Chris said he would.

So Chris and the dragon walked together. They
went to the playground, which was full of children
and full of mothers watching their children. When
the children saw the dragon, they ran to their
mothers, and the mothers screamed, and a few even
fainted. But Chris said, "Please don't be afraid. My
friend Mortimer is harmless and also a vegetarian,
and he likes people." When the mothers and
children heard this, they stopped screaming and
fussing, and the children came closer and wanted to
play. But the mothers did not like even a harmless
dragon as a playmate.

"Maybe it has diseases," said one mother.

"And it is probably shedding," said another.

"No matter what he says, a dragon is a dragon,"
said a third.

"I don't think you can ever trust them," said a
fourth.

So the children were not allowed to play with
Chris and his friend Mortimer, the dragon. And all
the mothers said, "Get that dragon out of here,
please."

10

11

So Christopher and Mortimer left the playground and were very sad.

Chris said, "I hope your feelings are not hurt, but people are very funny about dragons."

"I have noticed that," said Mortimer, with a sad green smile.

"Where do you live, Mort?" asked Chris.

"Nowhere. In fact, I am homeless," answered Mortimer.

"Then you can come live with me," said Chris, and he hoped that his mother would not say no.

"My mother might say no, but I will tell her you are my friend," said Chris.

It was a long way to the house where Chris lived.

"We will take the bus," said Chris, and Mortimer was delighted because he had never been in a bus before.

But when the bus stopped, the driver said, "Sorry, no dragons are allowed in the bus," and he drove off.

"We will take the ferry," said Chris.

But the ferry captain said, "Sorry, no dragons are allowed on the ferry."

"We will walk and cross over the bridge," said
Chris.

But cars zoomed by, and drivers honked their
horns, and a policeman came and said, "Get out of
here, or I'll have you arrested. No dragons are
allowed in the streets or on bridges."

15

Then Mortimer suggested that perhaps they had better fly.

"Can you really fly?" asked Chris.

"Of course," said Mortimer.

"Then why didn't you say so from the beginning?" asked Chris.

"I just wanted to be like everybody else. My mother always told me not to be a show-off if I wanted people to like me," answered Mortimer, and he spread open his two wings, which looked like two green half-umbrellas.

So they flew together to the house where Chris lived. Below, the cars were bumper to bumper, and the drivers looked up with envy. "That's the way to do it," said the drivers as they honked their horns at one another.

Chris entered the house first and said hello to his
mother and asked if he could bring in a friend.
His mother said yes, but when she saw Mortimer,
she said, "Get him out of here. No dragons in my
kitchen, no dragons in my house, please."
So poor Mortimer had to wait outside while
Chris begged his mother to let his friend
stay. Chris' mother kept saying no, no
and where would the dragon sleep,
and what would he eat, and who
would clean up the scales, and
so forth. But Chris promised that
he would take care of everything

18

and pick up scales off the rug with the vacuum cleaner if necessary. At last Chris' mother agreed reluctantly to let Mortimer stay, but for only one night.

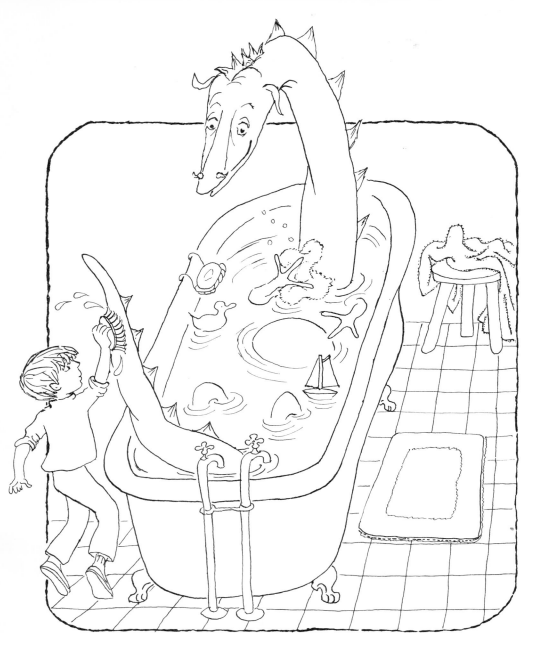

"Sorry you had to wait," said Chris to Mortimer,
"but my mother is afraid of dragons."

Christopher's mother made Mortimer take a bath,
and he washed off a few loose scales and looked
better.

Then they had some supper and went to bed.
But the bed was too small for both, and Mortimer
was all spikes and angles. So Chris slept on the
floor in his sleeping bag, which was used for
camping vacations.

21

The next day Chris' mother said, "Today is the day of the big parade, and the mayor and all the important townspeople and maybe even the governor will be there, and you'd better keep that dragon out of sight."

"Oh, Mother, he is quite harmless and also a vegetarian, and he likes people," said Chris.

"That has nothing to do with it. I want that dragon out of the house and out of sight," said Chris' mother.

When he heard these words, Mortimer crawled into a corner and sobbed quietly. He whispered sadly to himself, "I may be a dragon, but I have feelings . . . and I like people in spite of everything . . . Oh, how I wish they would like me too . . . sob . . . sob."

Chris comforted Mortimer as well as he could and then decided to take him back to the park, to the large rock where he had found him and where no one was around. Before leaving the house, Chris had to get his umbrella and rubbers and a raincoat because his mother had heard on the radio that it was going to rain.

"What a shame if it rains," said Chris' mother,
"for the parade and the mayor and the important
townspeople and maybe the governor, and especially
for the fireworks tonight."

23

"I wish people would like me better," said
Mortimer again, as they were on their way to the
park. They did not take a bus; they did not take
a ferry; they did not walk on a bridge. They flew.
They flew so low that they could see all the
preparations for the big parade that was soon to
begin. People were putting garlands around
lamp posts. Policemen were clearing the streets of
cars and buses. Children holding little flags lined
the curbs to wave at the mayor and the important
townspeople and maybe the governor as they went
by on their way to the reviewing stand. At last

Chris and Mortimer arrived at their destination. But the quiet spot was not quiet anymore. Many people were milling around.

"What is everybody doing?" asked Chris.

"We're getting the fireworks ready for tonight," said a man as he opened a big case of fireworks. More cases were opened, and the fireworks neatly arranged, ready for the evening display.

26

Then a man with a beard noticed Mortimer. "What is that dragon doing here?" said the man with the beard. "You'd better remove him before a policeman comes along."

"Oh, please," said Chris, "this is my friend Mortimer, and he is harmless and also a vegetarian, and he likes people, and he would love to watch the parade and see the mayor and the important townspeople and maybe the governor and the fireworks this evening."

"Well, all right," said the man with the beard. "Hide him behind some bushes, but be sure no one sees him, or I'll lose my job."

So they hid Mortimer.

Then the mayor appeared and all the important townspeople and also the governor. They rode in open cars up the avenue, and the people cheered and threw bits of paper from windows as a sign of friendship, and children waved their flags.

The mayor and the governor and the important townspeople sat in the reviewing stand under the red, white, and blue canopy, and the parade began.

30

The parade was very exciting with floats and bands and all sorts of marchers, but Mortimer was hidden in the bushes and could see only little bits of it.

Near the end of the parade heavy black clouds
began to gather, and everyone looked at the sky
and hoped it would not rain. But just as the parade
ended, it began to rain. It rained, and then it

THE SPIRIT OF .76

33

poured. The governor and the mayor and the important townspeople huddled under their red, white, and blue canopy, which sagged in the middle and dripped through a crack. People in the street opened their umbrellas. But no one went home. Everybody gathered in the park to see the fireworks display.

The people in charge of the fireworks tried to set them off, and the man with the beard, who was the boss, gave orders that no one could hear because of the rain, and he lost his temper because nothing happened. The fireworks did not go off.

34

They were soaked by the rain. The flames of the
matches sizzled and died. People were waiting
in the rain. The governor became impatient
and started to tap his fingers on the edge of the
railing. The important townspeople fidgeted, and
the mayor was embarrassed and got red in the face
and pulled at his collar, which was too tight.

35

The man with the beard was wringing his hands and saying, "It's my fault, and I know I'll lose my job."

The rain stopped but the fireworks still did not go off. They were just as wet as ever.

Then Mortimer came out from the bushes and said politely, "Please permit me to try." The crowd around the fireworks stepped back and watched in amazement as Mortimer blew himself up, puffed out his cheeks, and breathed a hot cloud of air that dried out the wet fireworks in one second. Then he spouted little flames, which set off the fireworks, not all at once, but one by one.

There were rockets that shot straight up and
then burst into thousands and thousands of falling
stars — red, green, blue, every color. Then there were
whirly ones and wiggly ones that looked like funny
little fireworms twisting in the sky. And there were

38

more and more, and then, at the end, after much
crackling and sputtering, there was a Niagara Falls
bigger than the real one and also an American
flag.

It was a splendid display.

39

The governor wished to congratulate the mayor and the important townspeople for the parade, and he especially wished to thank the people in charge of the fireworks. The man with the beard came forward and said, "Sir, we owe the success of the fireworks display to this distinguished gentleman by my side." And he presented Mortimer to the governor, the mayor, and the important townspeople.

The governor expressed deep gratitude to Mortimer. He said he was proud to have in his state a citizen who had served above and beyond the call of duty. He shook Mortimer's hand so hard that one scale fell off. A little girl picked it up immediately to put it in her scrapbook. Then the mayor expressed his gratitude, too, and he gave Mortimer a red, white, and blue ribbon for actions above and beyond the call of duty and shook his hand so hard that a few more scales fell off and were immediately picked up by the children for their scrapbooks. And some of the girls asked Mortimer for his autograph.

And that was not all. Mortimer was carried in triumph twice around the park, while people cheered and children waved sparklers and also their small flags, which were still damp from the rain. Finally, Mortimer was appointed assistant commissioner of parks and given as a residence the large rock he liked so well. So from then on, Mortimer could spend all his time in the park among the people and children whom he liked and who from then on liked him back.

43

When the weather was good, Mortimer and Chris
had picnics in the park, and Chris' mother made
special vegetarian cookies for Mortimer. When the
weather was very bad, Mortimer came to stay with
Chris. They played cards and other games, and at
bedtime Chris' mother usually read them a story,
but never a fairy tale with dragons. Fairy tales do
not always tell nice things about dragons, and
Mortimer's feelings might have been hurt.

And in the early spring, when the children came to the pond but the water was still too cold for swimming, Mortimer just puffed himself up and blew into the pond, and, bang, the water was as warm as the water of a bathtub. And the children could go swimming although it was only April. Everybody said that Mortimer was the most popular assistant commissioner of parks that ever was. And they were right.

219114

Vasiliu
Mortimer, the friendly
dragon